Picture Book Studio

The Brothers Grimm

JACK IN LUCK

Illustrated by Eve Tharlet

Translated and adapted by Anthea Bell

When Jack had served his master seven years, he said,
"Master, my time is up. I'm off home to my mother,
so give me my wages."

"You've served me well," said his master,
"so you shall be well paid."
And he gave Jack a lump of gold as big as his head.

Jack took a handkerchief out of his pocket,
wrapped the gold in it, put it over his shoulder,
and set off for home.

As he went on his way,
 he saw a man trotting along on a lively horse.
"Oh, how nice it must be to ride a horse!" said Jack.

 The horseman stopped and asked,
"Why are you traveling on foot, then?"

"I have to," said Jack. "This lump is so heavy!
 It may be made of gold,
 but it weighs me down."

"I'll tell you what," said the horseman.
"Let's swap. I'll give you my horse,
 and you give me your gold."

"By all means," said Jack,
"but I can tell you it's a terrible weight!"

 The horseman dismounted, took the gold,
 helped Jack up, gave him the reins and said,
"If you want to go fast,
 just click your tongue and say, *Gee up!*"

 So off rode Jack, happy as a lark.

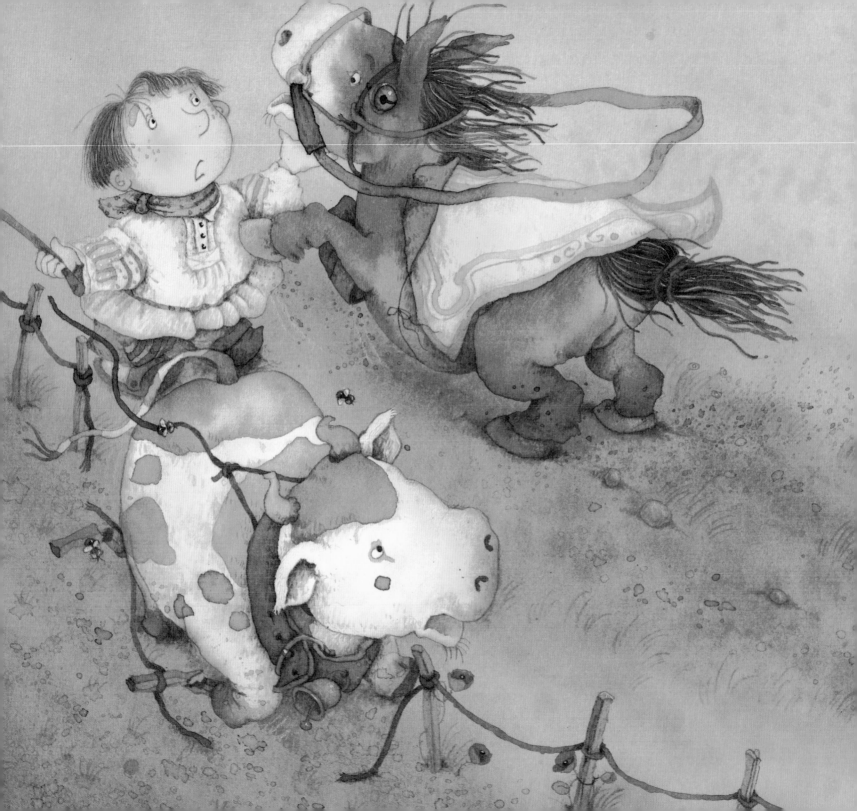

After a while Jack wanted to go faster,
so he clicked his tongue and said, "Gee up!"
The horse broke into a fast trot, and threw Jack off.
The horse would have run away,
but a farmer came down the road
driving a cow, and stopped it.

Jack got to his feet again, in a bad temper.
"Riding's no fun on a nag like that," he said.
"Your cow's better. She walks quietly along,
and gives milk for making butter and cheese.
I wish I had a cow like that!"

"Well," said the farmer, "if you like,
I'll swap my cow for your horse."

Jack happily agreed,
and the farmer mounted the horse
and rode away in haste.

Jack drove his cow along the road,
thinking of the good bargain he had struck.
"Once I have a bit of bread–
and I'm sure to have bread–
I can eat butter and cheese whenever I like.
When I'm thirsty I can milk my cow
and drink the milk. What more could I want?"

On coming to an inn he stopped,
ate everything he had with him–
both his lunch and his dinner–
and bought half a glass of beer
with the very last of his money.
Then he drove his cow on toward
the village where his mother lived.

It became very hot around noon
and Jack was very thirsty.

"I'll milk my cow," thought Jack,

"and drink the milk."

But however hard he tried he couldn't milk her.
And he was so clumsy that in the end she kicked him,
and he fell over and was left in a daze.

Luckily a butcher was coming down the road
with a young pig in a wheelbarrow.

"Whatever are you doing?" he cried,
helping poor Jack up again. So Jack told his story.

The butcher gave him a drink of water.
"That cow won't give you any milk," he said.
"She's an old beast, fit for nothing
but slaughter."

"Fancy that!" said Jack. "Who'd have thought it?
Still, it's a good thing to have a beast to slaughter at home.
There'd be plenty of meat, but I don't like cow beef much.
It's too tough for me.
I wish I had a young pig like yours instead–
and just think of the sausages!"

"Well, Jack," said the butcher,
"I'll swap you my pig for your cow, if you like."

"That's kind of you," said Jack, giving him the cow.
He took the pig out of the barrow
and holding its rope he went on his way,
thinking how well
everything turned out for him.

Soon he met a young man with a fine white goose under his arm.
Jack told the tale of his good luck.

The young man said he was taking the goose
to a christening party.
"Feel how heavy she is," he said.

"Yes, she's a good weight," said Jack,
"but my pig's not bad either."

The young man looked at the pig, and said,
"There's been a pig stolen
in the village I've just left.
I'm very much afraid
it's this one!
They're after the thief!"

Jack was scared.
"Take my pig,"
he begged,
"and give me
your goose."

"Very well," said the young man.
So he took the rope,
and hurried off with the pig.

Jack went on his way,
with the goose under his arm.
"That was a good bargain,"
said he to himself.
"First I'll have a good roast goose,
then all the fat that runs out of it,
and last of all the fine white feathers
to stuff my pillow.
Won't my mother be pleased!"

In the last village, Jack met a knife grinder,
who asked where he had bought the goose.

"I swapped it for a pig," said Jack.
   "Where did you get the pig?"
"I swapped it for a cow."
   "Where did you get the cow?"
"I swapped it for a horse."
   "Where did you get the horse?"
"I swapped it for a lump of gold."
   "Where did you get the lump of gold?"
"I swapped it for seven years' work."

"If you were a knife grinder, "said the man,
 you'd always have money in your pocket."
And he offered Jack a whetstone.

Jack took it, gave the man the goose,
and went happily on his way,
thinking how good it would be
always to have money in his pocket.

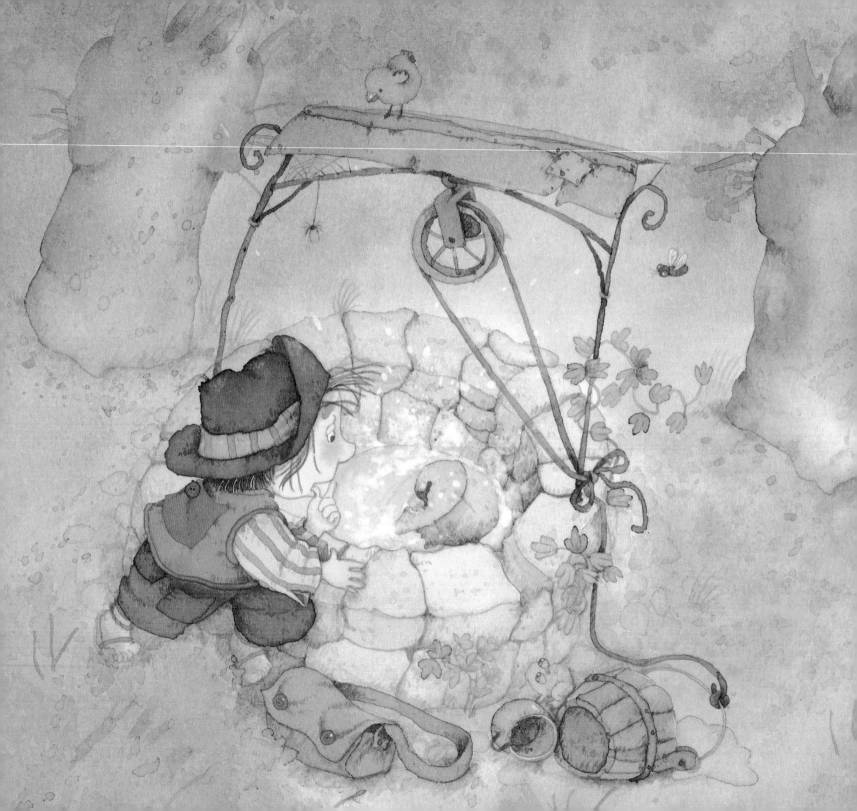

The knife grinder had given Jack another
stone too, an ordinary, heavy one,
saying he could sleep on it,
or knock bent nails straight on it,
any time he liked.
"I was born under a lucky star," thought Jack.
"Everything I wish for comes true!"

Soon he felt tired and hungry.
The stones weighed heavier and heavier,
and he couldn't help thinking
how pleasant it would be
if he didn't have to carry them just now.
At a snail's pace, he made his way to a well
to rest and drink cool water.

He put the stones down on its rim,
and as he bent to drink,
they both fell into the well.

Seeing them fall, Jack jumped for joy,
and then knelt down and thanked God
with tears in his eyes for ridding him
of those heavy stones.
They had only been a burden to him.
"There can't be a luckier man than I
under the sun!" cried Jack.

And light of heart, without a care in the world,
he ran all the way home to his mother.

A Michael Neugebauer Book.
Copyright © 1992 by Neugebauer Press, Salzburg, Austria.
Published by Picture Book Studio Ltd., Saxonville, Massachusetts.
Distributed in the United States by Simon & Schuster.
Distributed in Canada by Vanwell Publishing, St. Catharines, Ontario.
All rights reserved.
Printed in Hong Kong.

Library of Congress Cataloging-in-Publication Data
Hans im Glück. English.
Jack in luck / written by the Brothers Grimm;
illustrated by Eve Tharlet: translated by Anthea Bell.
p. cm.
Translation of Hans im Glück.
Summary: When his seven years' wages in gold proves too heavy to carry,
Jack trades it in for one thing after another until he arrives home empty-handed
but convinced he is a lucky man.
ISBN 0-88708-249-1 : $14.95
[1. Fairy tales. 2. Folklore—Germany.] 1. Grimm, Jacob, 1785-1863.
II. Grimm, Wilhelm, 1786-1859. III. Tharlet, Eve, ill. IV. Title.
PZ8.H195   1992
398.21—dc20   92-7102
CIP
AC

Look for these other Picture Book Studio titles illustrated by Eve Tharlet:
Little Pig, Big Trouble by Eve Tharlet
Christmas Won't Wait by Eve Tharlet
Little Pig, Bigger Trouble by Eve Tharlet
Simon & the Holy Night by Eve Tharlet
The Brave Little Tailor by The Brothers Grimm
Dizzy From Fools by M.L. Miller
The Princes and the Pea by H.C. Andersen